KING OF ROME

DAVE SUDBURY

ILLUSTRATED BY HANS SAEFKOW

SIMPLY READ BOOKS

In the West End of Derby
lived a working man.

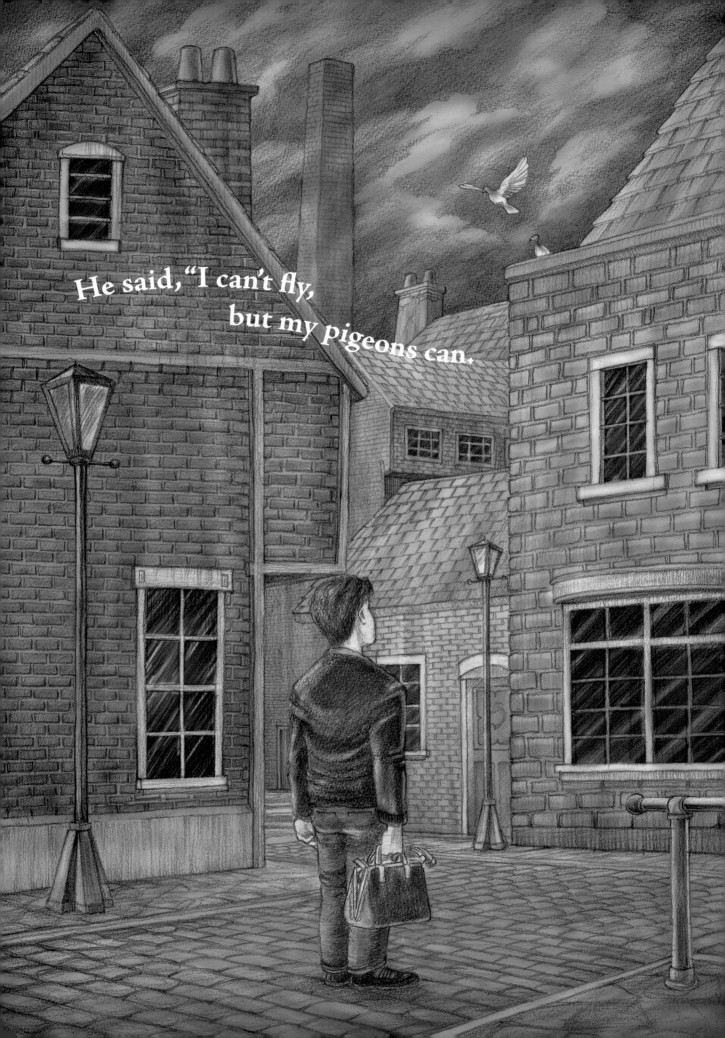

He said, "I can't fly, but my pigeons can.

When I set them free,
it's just like part of me
gets lifted up on shining wings."

Charlie Hudson's pigeon loft was down the yard of a rented house in Brook Street where life was hard.

But Charlie, he had a dream;
by nineteen thirteen,
Charlie bred a pigeon that made
his dream come true.

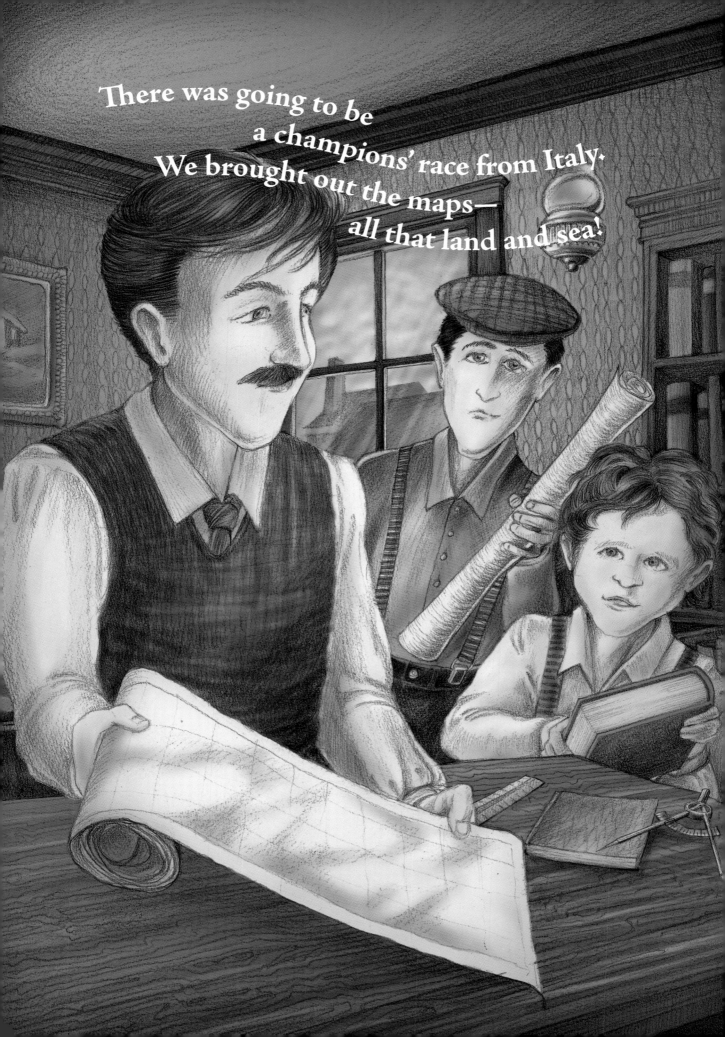

There was going to be
a champions' race from Italy.
We brought out the maps—
all that land and sea!

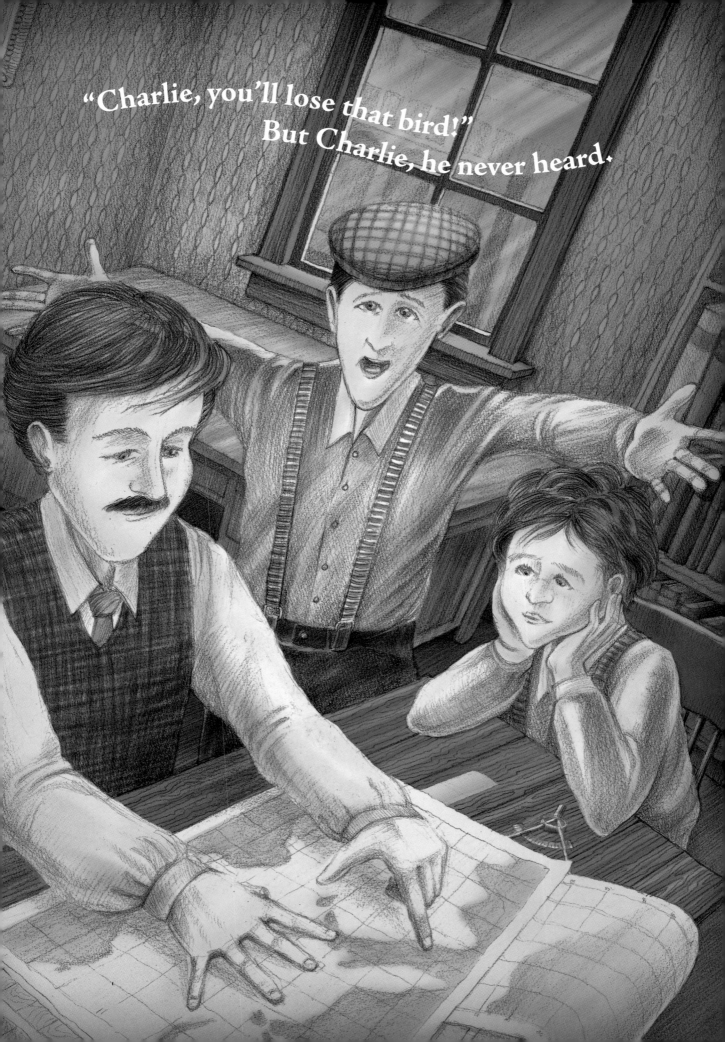

He put it in a basket
and sent it off to Rome.

On the day of the big race,
a storm blew in.

A thousand birds were swept away and were never seen again.

"Charlie, we told you so.
Surely by now you'd know.

"Yeah, I know, but I had to try.
You see, a man can crawl around,
or he can learn to fly."

And when you live round here,
the ground can seem awful near."

"Sometimes I need a lift from victory."

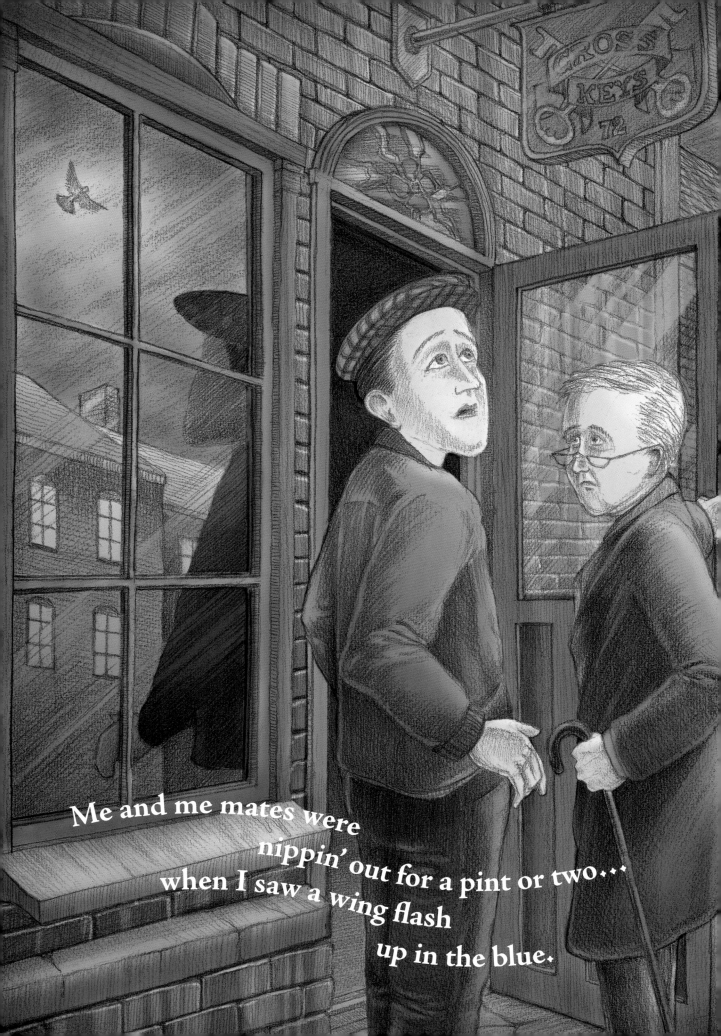

Me and me mates were nippin' out for a pint or two... when I saw a wing flash up in the blue.

"Charlie! It's the King of Rome! He's come back to his West End home!"

"Come outside quick—
he's perched upon your roof."

"Come on down, your Majesty.
I knew you'd make it back to me."

"Come on down, my lovely one.
You made my dream come true."

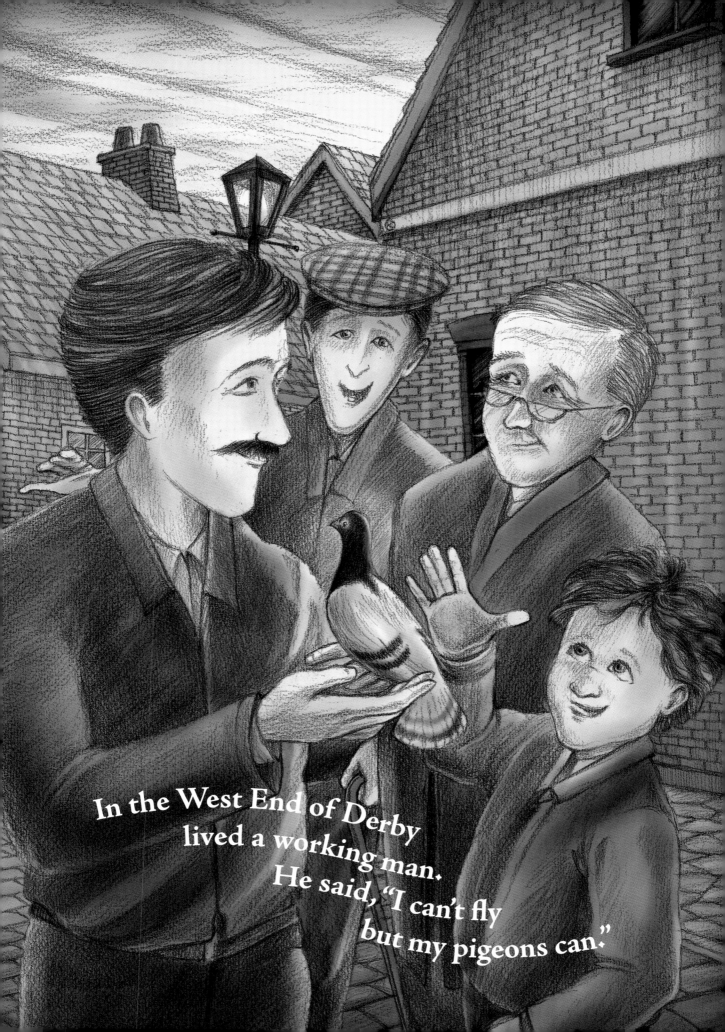

In the West End of Derby
lived a working man.
He said, "I can't fly
but my pigeons can."

"When I set them free,
it's like part of me
gets lifted up on shining wings."

Published in 2008 by Simply Read Books
www.simplyreadbooks.com

Text copyright ©2008 Dave Sudbury
Illustrations copyright ©2008 Hans Saefkow

Library and Archives Canada Cataloguing in Publication

Sudbury, Dave, 1943-
King of Rome / Dave Sudbury ; illustrator, Hans Saefkow.

ISBN 987-1-894965-94-1

1. Hudson, Charlie—Juvenile fiction. Racing pigeons—Juvenile fiction.
I.Saefkow, Hans, 1964 - II. Title.

PZ7.S935Ki 2007   j823'.92   C2007-905126-X

Book design by Studio: Blackwell, Kelsey Blackwell with Alex Nelson.
Printed in Singapore

We gratefully acknowledge the support of the Canada Council for the Arts and
the BC Arts Council for our publishing program.

10 9 8 7 6 5 4 3 2 1

Dave Sudbury was born 1943 in Derby, an industrial town in the English Midlands. He left school at 16 and started work in a local factory as an apprentice pipefitter. When he had served his time he went working around the country in power stations and on the North Sea gas pipelines. Later on, when he'd settled down, he wrote songs about his life and experiences and sang them around the local folk clubs. He recorded them on a CD called 'The King of Rome'— Songs of Dave Sudbury. The title song, 'The King of Rome', has been recorded by numerous singers and used in a film by the iconic English film director Ken Russell, 'In Search of the English Folksong'. Dave now works in a psychiatric hospital facilitating music groups and lives in the United Kingdom.

Hans Saefkow is a graduate of the Ontario College of Art and was a BCYCNA editorial cartoonist of the year. Currently he is a set designer at the Theatre North West in Prince George, British Columbia. This is his first book.